ALSO BY ERROL LLOYD

Nini at Carnival

for Asana

British Library Cataloguing
in Publication Data
Lloyd, Errol
Nandy's bedtime.
I. Title
823′.914 [J] PZ7
ISBN 0-370-30395-4

Copyright © Errol Lloyd 1982
Printed in Belgium for
The Bodley Head Children's Books
an imprint of The Random Century Group Ltd
20 Vauxhall Bridge Road, London SW1V 2SA
by Proost International Book Production
First published 1982
Reprinted 1991

Nandy's Bedtime
Errol Lloyd

THE BODLEY HEAD

London

Nandy is playing, but it is getting
late and soon it will be her bedtime.

"Come on, Nandy," says Mummy,
"let's pack away these toys."

Nandy helps Mummy cook the dinner.

"Mmm, very good, Nandy," says Daddy. "You can help me cook tomorrow."

"Time for your bath now, Nandy," says Daddy, "but clean your teeth first."

Nandy enjoys splashing
in the bath. . .

and blowing bubbles, too.

Daddy lifts Nandy
out and wraps a big
bath towel round her.
Teddy is dripping wet.

Daddy helps Nandy
to put on her pyjamas.

Then Mummy reads her a story,
until it's time to go to sleep.

"Good-night, Mummy.
Good-night, Daddy."

Nandy gives Bimbo and Teddy
a good-night kiss, too.
Good-night, Nandy. Sleep tight.